LEVEL 2 READER

#34

SCOOBY-DOO!

GIDDYUP, SCOOBY-DOO!

By Lee Howard
Illustrated by Alcadia SNC

SCHOLASTIC INC.

ISBN 978-0-545-93226-4

10 9 8 7 6 5 4 3 2 1 16 17 18 19 20

Printed in the U.S.A. 40

First printing 2016

Scooby-Doo and the kids from Mystery, Inc. were spending a week at Tumbleweed Ranch.

"Like, this place is so cool!" said Shaggy.

"Reah!" agreed Scooby.

The ranch's owner, Slim Jim, came over to greet the gang.

"Welcome to Tumbleweed Ranch!" he said.

“I hope you enjoy your stay here, but you’ve come at a bad time,” said Slim Jim. “Someone has been stealing my horses!”

“We’ll help you find them,” said Fred. “We’re good at solving mysteries.”

“We need to get close to the horses,” said Velma.

“Why don’t you take our rodeo clown class?” suggested Slim Jim.

“This is Jingles,” said Slim Jim. “He’ll show you the ropes!”

Scooby and Shaggy were great at playing the fool.

"You two will make perfect rodeo clowns," said Jingles.

"Did you hear that, Scooby?" said Shaggy. "Like, we're going to be clowns!"

"Roh roy!" said Scooby.

First, Jingles taught Scooby and Shaggy how to rope a steer.

Shaggy roped Scooby.

Then Scooby roped Shaggy!

The rest of the gang watched and clapped.
"Jinkies," said Velma. "What are those two up to now?"
"Acting like clowns," said Daphne, laughing.

After class, Slim Jim introduced the gang to a tall cowboy.

"This is my neighbor, Ray Bob Gilley," he said.

"Howdy," said Ray Bob.

"Ray Bob used to own this ranch and all the horses," said Slim Jim.

Ray Bob nodded. "I like to come back and visit sometimes."

That night, the gang made a campfire.
Then they heard strange noises.
"Did you hear that?" asked Velma.
"It sounds like horses whinnying," said Fred.

The gang ran to the stables. Slim Jim met them there.

"Two horses are missing!" he said.

"Maybe the thief left a clue," said Velma.

Velma and Daphne found streaks of white goo on the ground. "What's this?" asked Daphne.

"White makeup," said Fred. "And yarn!"
"Hmm," said Velma. "Someone has been clowning around in here!"

The next day, Jingles taught Scooby and Shaggy how to juggle.

At least, he tried to teach them!

After class, Fred and Daphne followed Jingles back to the stables.

Jingles patted one of the horses.

"See you later, Midnight," he whispered.

Fred and Daphne
hurried back to the gang.

Scooby, Shaggy, and Velma were sitting around the campfire, toasting marshmallows.

"Gang, it's time to set a trap," said Fred. "We need to catch the horse thief in the act."

"Ruh-roh," said Scooby.

"Like, what kind of trap?" asked Shaggy.

"We'll camp out at the stables tonight," said Daphne.

The gang went to their tents to wait for the thief.

Soon Scooby and Shaggy fell sound asleep…

Until a big, scary shadow appeared outside their tent!

"AHHHHHHH!" cried Shaggy.

He and Scooby slid deep into their sleeping bags.

"Get your lasso, Scoob," whispered Shaggy. "It's time to catch that crook!"

Outside, Scooby and Shaggy saw a dark figure leading a horse away from the stables.

Scooby threw his lasso at the shadow.
He roped something!
"Ree-haw!" Scooby cheered.

Fred, Daphne, and Velma heard the noise and came running.

So did Jingles and Slim Jim.

"We caught the horse thief!" Shaggy said.

"I guess I taught you something right," said Jingles, grinning.

“Let’s see who’s hiding under this clown wig,” said Fred.

Daphne pulled off the thief’s wig.

“Ray Bob Gilley!” the gang gasped.

The gang took Ray Bob to the sheriff's jailhouse.

"I wanted to steal back my old horses," said Ray Bob.

"You dressed up like a clown so Slim Jim would think I was the thief," said Jingles.

"I would've gotten away with it if it hadn't been for you meddling kids!" said Ray Bob.

"You'll have plenty of time to clown around in jail," said Velma.

The next day, the gang enjoyed their last barbecue.

"Anyone want to round up a few prairie dogs?" asked Jingles.

"Like, we're more interested in hot dogs!" said Shaggy.

"Rup," agreed Scooby. "Scooby-Dooby-Doo!"